THE
CHANUKKAH
GUEST

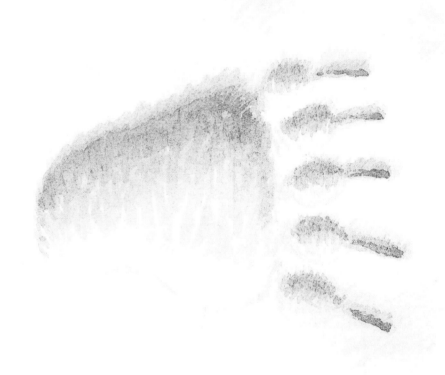

THE CHANUKKAH GUEST

Eric A. Kimmel

illustrated by
Giora Carmi

Holiday House/New York

Bubba —"Grandmother" or "Granny."

dreidel — a four-sided top. The letters on each of the four sides stand for Hebrew words meaning, "A Great Miracle Happened There."

latke — a potato pancake, usually eaten with apple-sauce, jam, or sour cream.

menorah—"candlestick." The Chanukkah menorah has holders for nine candles, eight for each of the eight days of Chanukkah, and an additional one for the "shammes" or "servant" candle which is used to light the others.

This story first appeared in
Cricket, the Magazine for Children

Text copyright © 1988 by Eric A. Kimmel
Illustrations copyright © 1990 by Giora Carmi
All rights reserved
Manufactured in China

Library of Congress Cataloging-in-Publication Data
Kimmel, Eric A.
    The Chanukkah guest / written by Eric A. Kimmel ; illustrated
by Giora Carmi.
        p.   cm.
    Summary: On the first night of Chanukkah, Old Bear wanders
into Bubba Brayna's house and receives a delicious helping of
potato latkes when she mistakes him for the rabbi.
    ISBN 0-8234-0788-8
    [1. Hanukkah—Fiction. 2. Bears—Fiction.] I. Carmi, Giora,
ill. II. Title.
PZ7.K5648Cg 1990 [E]—dc20   89-20073 CIP
    ISBN 0-8234-0978-3 (pbk.)
ISBN-13: 978-0-8234-0788-0 (hardcover)   ISBN-10: 0-8234-0788-8 (hardcover)
ISBN-13: 978-0-8234-0978-5 (paperback)   ISBN-10: 0-8234-0978-3 (paperback)

For Aunt Florence and Aunt Ann

E.A.K.

To my family, who bears with me

G.C.

Old Bear roused himself from his winter sleep. He yawned a gigantic yawn. Then he stretched himself all over. Finally he poked his nose outside his den. A soft blanket of deep snow covered the ground. Spring was still many months away. Old Bear wrinkled his nose. What was that delicious smell? It smelled like something to eat, which reminded Old Bear that it had been months since he had eaten anything. Old Bear's empty stomach rumbled. He shook himself all over, then lumbered out of his den to follow the delicious smell.

Bubba Brayna took the last potato latke from the pan and put it in the oven with the others. The latkes would stay warm in there until her guests arrived. Bubba Brayna was ninety-seven years old and did not hear or see as well as she used to, but she still made the best potato latkes in the village. Every year at Chanukkah time all her friends made their way through the snow to her little house on the edge of the forest. How they loved those latkes! Bubba Brayna always made plenty. But tonight, on the first night of Chanukkah, she made twice as many as usual. Tonight was special. Tonight the rabbi was coming.

Bubba Brayna put on a clean apron and set the table. She filled a bowl with nuts for the dreidel game. Kitzel the cat rubbed against her ankles as she bustled around the kitchen. One last chore: the candles for the menorah. Bubba Brayna went to get them. Just then she heard a knock at the door.

It wasn't exactly a knock; more like a soft thumping. "My guests must be early," Bubba Brayna said. She opened the door. The cat hissed and dived under the table.

"Why, Rabbi, how nice to see you!" Bubba Brayna exclaimed.

"Grrrrumph," growled Old Bear.

"And Happy Chanukkah to you, too. Please come in."

Old Bear lumbered into the house. He shook the snow from his fur.

"I'll take your coat, Rabbi. My, how thick it is! It must be very cold outside." Bubba Brayna tugged at Old Bear's fur.

"Grrrrrowwww!" Old Bear roared.

"Oh, you prefer to leave your coat on? Well, that's all right. It is a bit chilly in here. Come into the kitchen. I've set the table for a lovely Chanukkah evening."

Old Bear followed Bubba Brayna into the kitchen. The delicious smells made his nose twitch.

"Rrrrumph!"

"Thank you, Rabbi. How kind of you to say that. The latkes will taste even better than they smell."

Old Bear followed his nose to the oven.
"RRROOOOWRGH!"
"Rabbi, I'm surprised at you! You know we don't eat until we light the menorah."
"Grrrrr!"
"That's all right. I know you were teasing. I'll light the candles. Will you say the blessings?"
"Rrrumph."

Bubba Brayna struck a match and lit the shammes candle. Then she lit the one for the first night. Old Bear muttered and growled.

"Rrrumph . . . grrroooowr . . . rrrrr . . ."

" '. . . who has kept us, preserved us, and sustained us to this time.' Oh, Rabbi, you say the blessings so beautifully!"

Bubba Brayna pulled out a chair. Old Bear sat down. "Let's play dreidel. I have some nuts we can play with." Old Bear's nose twitched. He cracked a nut in his teeth.

"Rabbi, you won't have any nuts for the game if you eat them all."

"Rrrummmr," growled Old Bear.

"Don't worry. I have more nuts if you need them." Bubba Brayna gave the dreidel a spin. Old Bear sniffed at the little top as it whirled around. It stopped on the letter 'nun.'

"Nothing. We spin again." Bubba Brayna spun the dreidel once more. This time it stopped on the letter 'gimel.'

"I win!" Bubba Brayna swept the nuts into her apron.

"RRRROWRRRR!" Old Bear roared.

"Don't be angry, Rabbi. It's only a game. Here!" She tossed him a nut. Old Bear caught it in his paws, cracked it handily, then begged for more.

"No Rabbi, no more nuts. It's time for dinner."

Old Bear snuffled and grumbled. Bubba Brayna opened the oven door and took out a platter piled high with steaming potato latkes. Old Bear's nose twitched as she set them on the table. "Do you prefer your latkes with sour cream or jam?"

"Rrrrughrrr!" Old Bear growled.

"Jam. I thought so." Bubba Brayna smeared five big latkes with jam and stacked them on Old Bear's plate. Old Bear snuffled with pleasure as he gobbled the latkes down.

Bubba Brayna laughed. "You should use a fork. You have jam all over your beard." She wet a towel and wiped Old Bear's face. "I must tell you, Rabbi. You eat just like a bear."

"GRRROARRRURRRR!!!"
" 'I'm hungry as a bear, so I eat like one.' I can see that!" Bubba Brayna chuckled.

Old Bear ate and ate until all the latkes were gone. He licked jam and sour cream from his muzzle and his paws. Then Old Bear began to feel drowsy. He yawned. His great head flopped on Bubba Brayna's lap.

"Rabbi, you're sleepy. Who wouldn't be after such a meal? All the latkes are gone. It's time to go home. But before you leave I have a Chanukkah present for you." Bubba Brayna took out a red woolen scarf from the cupboard. She wrapped it around Old Bear's neck. "This scarf will keep you warm on the coldest nights. I knitted it myself."

"Grrrurrrrr." Old Bear licked Bubba Brayna's face. Bubba Brayna blushed. "Oh, Rabbi! At my age!"

Old Bear shuffled to the door. It was time to return to his den. He felt very sleepy. "Rrrrumph," he growled as he ambled off into the night. He turned around one more time before disappearing into the forest. "Rrrrumph."

"Good night to you, too, Rabbi! Happy Chanukkah!"

Bubba Brayna was washing the dishes when she heard another knock. "I wonder who that is?"

"Shalom, Bubba Brayna!" Her friends and neighbors stood at the door wishing her a happy Chanukkah.

"Shalom, everybody!" Bubba Brayna cried. "How nice to see you. Please come in. I'm sorry I don't have any more latkes. The rabbi came by. He ate them all."

"Bubba Brayna, don't you recognize me?" It was the rabbi.

"The rabbi couldn't have eaten the latkes," everyone said. "He was in the synagogue with us the whole time."

Bubba Brayna scratched her head in bewilderment. "Something strange is happening here. Rabbi, I think there is an imposter going around. He looks like you. He talks like you. He even has your beard."

Just then Esther and David, Bubba Brayna's two grand-children, cried, "Come look!" Everyone ran to the kitchen to see what was wrong. They found the floor covered with bear tracks.

"A bear! And I thought it was the rabbi." Bubba Brayna had to sit down. Soon she began to giggle. "That was a very clever bear . . . or a very foolish Bubba Brayna. Ah well, let the bear have a happy Chanukkah. I had a happy Chanukkah too. And so will you, my dear friends.

David, go bring some potatoes up from the cellar. Esther, get my grater and bowl. Everybody has to help. You too, Rabbi. But I promise there will soon be latkes for everyone!"

Deep in the forest Old Bear slumbered in his den. His stomach was full of potato latkes. The warm woolen scarf was wrapped snugly around his neck.

Pleasant dreams, Old Bear. And Happy Chanukkah.